D0515592

Piglette's
Perfect *Surprise*

by **Katelyn Aronson**

pictures by **Eva Byrne**

VIKING

The pasture may have been Piglette's home, but **Paris** was her playground. She visited practically every weekend to help out at the perfumery owned by Madame Paradee.

Madame's surprise birthday party was coming up, so Piglette perused the shops.

Only the perfect present will do! she thought.

When a warm vanilla scent curled around the corner,

she followed her snout . . .

. . . to the patisserie of Chef Pistache.

Today, it looked more like a flower shop!
Peonies sprouted from pastries.
Chrysanthemums cascaded from cakes.

Piglette poked her head in and sniffed.
A whiff of chocolate . . . a scent of
strawberry . . . a hint of hazelnut . . .

"Bonjour, Piglette!
Come taste the dream!
I made it all
with buttercream!"

"Merci!" said Piglette.
"It's too pretty to eat!" But she
nibbled anyway. "Mmm . . .
lavender-lemon?"

"Mais oui!" said Pistache.
"The sweet and the sour.
It's true what they say, then?
You know every flower?"
Chef needed help with new flavors.

"Of course!"
said Piglette. "I'd
love to help. If
you would help
me make the
perfect birthday
cake?"

"Deal!" Pistache said.
"C'est magnifique!
A partnership.
We start this week!"

Piglette picked plenty of posies to inspire Chef's buttercream bouquet. In exchange, he trained her in pastry-making.

Now, every night, she dreamed up the most delicious desserts for the big day.

But making them wasn't so easy.
Every teaspoon, tablespoon, and
temperature had to be
100 percent precise.

Otherwise, cookies crumbled.
Cakes came out like crêpes.

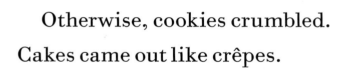

Oh, *piddle!*

*I can't disappoint
Madame Paradee on
her special day.*

Piglette practiced and practiced. . . .

When her pastries were practically perfect,
Pistache had to leave for a wedding.

"You've tested all my recipes.
*Now pick **just one** that's sure to please."*

But Piglette couldn't pick just one.

On the eve of Madame Paradee's party, she stood alone in the kitchen.

"Oh! The pressure!" she whispered.

She put on her apron, took a deep breath . . .

and soon,
sweet smells swirled around the room.

After a sleepless night, Piglette arrived at the Palace Hotel, with something top-secret in tow.

Everyone whispered
impatiently, until Madame
Paradee pranced in. . . .

"Surprise!"
everyone shouted.

A tower of treats—
ALL the treats—
pointed to the heavens.
Ooh la las gave way
to applause.

"A triumph!"

"A masterpiece!"

"Perfection!"
cried Madame Paradee.
"I'm tickled pink!"
Piglette had never
been so proud.

...Plip!

...Plop!

In the warmth of the day, her tower teetered.
It sagged. . . . It slid. . . . Its pieces began
pelting the partygoers!

Plip! . . . *Plop!* . . .

PLOOP!

Amid the pandemonium, Piglette
panicked and made her escape.

Madame Paradee found Piglette
in the pantry.

"My poor Piglette!"

Piglette whimpered. "Your present
was supposed to be ***perfect***."

"My petite," said Madame Paradee. "Handmade gifts are never *perfectly* perfect. Yet they're the most precious presents of all!"

"But the cake went . . . kaput!" said Piglette.

"*Pishposh.* Did you happen to *taste* it? Come, my dear. . . ."

Piglette's handiwork lay in a horrendous heap. But partygoers were pigging out! So she and Madame Paradee sampled for themselves. They licked lemon lilies. Crunched vanilla violets. Chewed chocolate chrysanthemums. Finally, Madame plucked a strawberry from the pile.

"Scrumptious!" said Madame.
"Strawberries have always been my favorite."

Piglette stared in surprise. She'd confectioned the most complicated of cakes without ever asking about Madame Paradee's favorite dessert. Strawberries.

As simple as that.

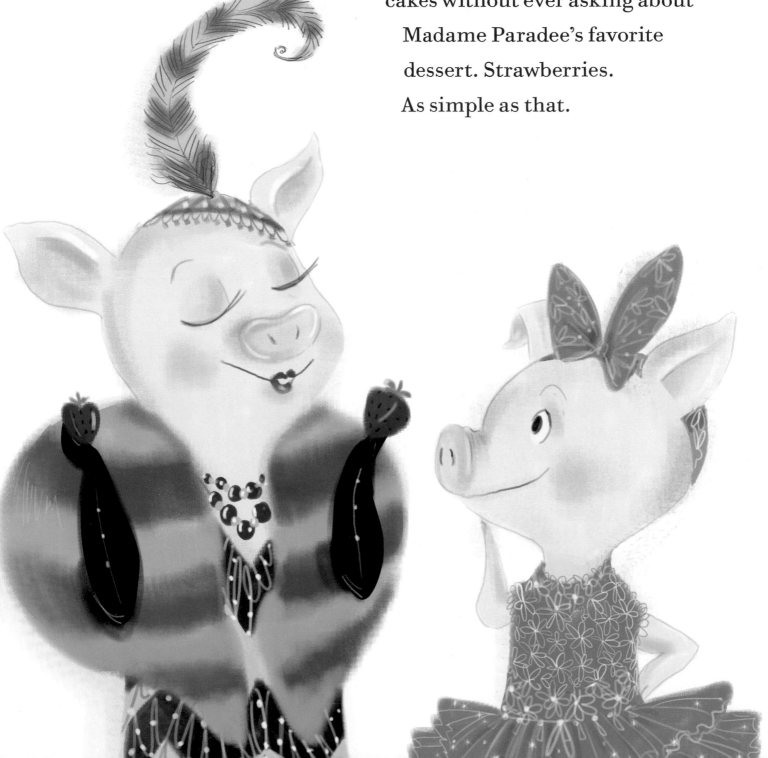

When Piglette returned home to the
pasture, she pondered . . .

I try so hard to make things "simply perfect."
But perhaps the best things are ***perfectly simple.***

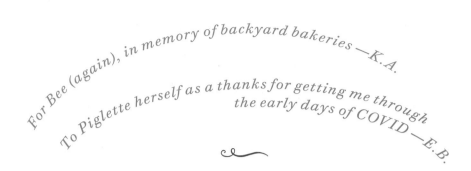

For Bee (again), in memory of backyard bakeries —K.A.

To Piglette herself as a thanks for getting me through
the early days of COVID —E.B.

VIKING

An imprint of Penguin Random House LLC, New York

First published in the United States of America by Viking,
an imprint of Penguin Random House LLC, 2021

Visit us online at penguinrandomhouse.com

LIBRARY OF CONGRESS CATALOGING-IN-PUBLICATION DATA IS AVAILABLE

Manufactured in China

ISBN 9780593204535

1   3   5   7   9   10   8   6   4   2

Set in Bodoni Six

The illustrations for this book were created digitally using Photoshop.